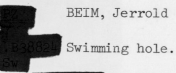

BEIM, Jerrold

Swimming hole.

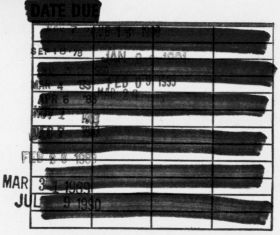

Swimming Hole

by JERROLD BEIM

Pictures by
LOUIS DARLING

WILLIAM MORROW & COMPANY
New York, 1950

14   15   75

For Bruce, Paul, Cole, the two Davids,
and all the gang at the swimming hole

Larry was eating his lunch.
"Larry! Come on! We're going
for a swim!" He heard the boys
calling from outside. His mother
opened the door. "Larry's not
finished yet. Come on in," she
said.

Larry's friends - Chris, Bob, Walt, and George - waited for him. His mother gave each of them an apple. "Don't go in the water for a while yet," she called as they started off.

They had fun on the way to the
swimming hole. They jumped
over a fire hydrant. They watched
furniture being moved into a new
house.

They looked into the window
of Mrs. Thomas' store.

Then they ran down the path
that led to the swimming hole.
"Come on in," other boys called.
The boys changed into trunks.
They hid their clothes under
some bushes and raced for the
water. "Last one in is a rotten
egg," Bob shouted.

There was plenty of room for
everyone in the swimming hole.

"We'd better go home!"
Chris said later. They found their

clothes under the bushes and put
them on. Then they started home.

They looked in the store window. They jumped over fire hydrants. "Look, a new boy's moved in there!" Larry said.

It was very hot the next day and the boys went swimming again. The new boy was in front of his house when they went by. "Can I go swimming with you?" he asked. "Yes, come on," everyone answered.

The new boy's name was Steve. When they reached the swimming hole, they put on their trunks. Steve was not a good swimmer, so he stayed out of the water most of the time. The hot sun beat down on him.

When it was time to go home, Larry picked up his clothes. He was surprised at what he saw!

"Look at mine, too!" Bob exclaimed. "Who did that?" "I did it!" Steve answered.

"You did it! What for?" Larry asked. "Because I don't like you!" Steve answered. "I don't want to play with anyone who's colored!"

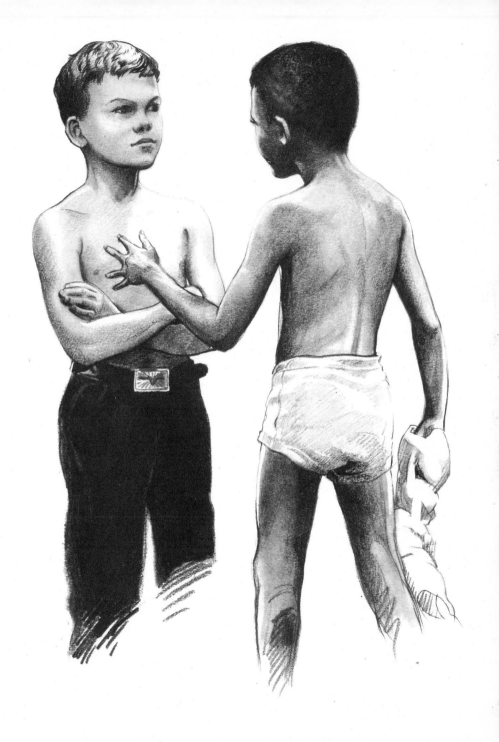

That made Larry mad. "I'm as good as you are!" he said. "You bet he is!" Chris added. "You go on home," Walt said to Steve. "We don't want you here!"

Larry watched Steve go. He saw that Steve looked red from being out in the sun all afternoon. "Say, look at Steve," Larry exclaimed. "Why don't we tell him we won't play with anyone that color?" The boys looked at Steve and laughed. "That's a good idea," they said.

They saw Steve on their way to the swimming hole the next day. He was as red as a boiled lobster. His face was red. His arms were red. Even his ears were red. "Going swimming?" Steve asked. "Yes, but you're not," Chris answered. "We don't want to play with anyone the color you are!"

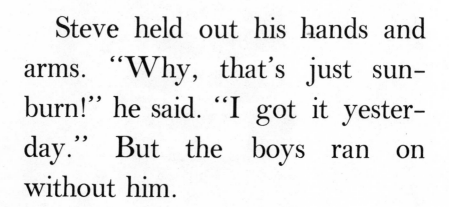

Steve held out his hands and arms. "Why, that's just sunburn!" he said. "I got it yesterday." But the boys ran on without him.

They looked back at Steve before they went down the path to the swimming hole. He was standing in front of Mrs. Thomas' store.

Steve was staring at himself in the window.

The boys played and swam in
the water. They saw Steve come
down the path, but no one paid
any attention to him.

After a while Larry got out of the water and stood on a rock. Then he turned and saw Steve standing beside him.

"Larry, I won't tie your clothes again," Steve said. "It doesn't matter what color people are."

"Of course it doesn't!" Larry answered. "Come on in the water. I'll teach you to swim!"

They all had a wonderful time
together.